ARE YOU A BIRD LIKE ME?

Written by
Noel Foy &
Nicholas Roberto

Illustrated by
Colleen Sgroi

Thanks to Chris, Michelle, Kerry, Margaret, Laurie, Marie, Jake, Nate, Max, Rob, Kristen, Trish and Nancy for their love, kindness and feedback.
So grateful you're in our nest!

Are You A Bird Like Me?
Story and Text Copyright 2022 Noel Foy and Nicholas Roberto
Illustration Copyright 2022 Colleen Sgroi

1 2 3 4 5 6 7 8 9 0

ISBN 978-1-62502-056-7

Library of Congress Control Number 2021922944

1. Friendship - Juvenile   2. Adventure - Juvenile   3. Diversity - Juvenile
4. Courage - Juvenile   5. Cooperation - Fiction

I. Foy, Noel II. Roberto, Nicholas III. Sgroi, Colleen

Published by Pear Tree Publishing
Bradford, MA

Pq
PEAR
TREE
PUBLISHING

For my family, you make my nest
bigger, brighter and better.
—Noel

For my daughter, Casey.
-- Nicholas

For my children, who have taught me so much about
courage, diversity and resilience.
— Colleen

This book belongs to:

At the tippy top of a tall-tall tree
there was a nest, and in that nest was an egg,
and in that egg was a baby bird named Sky.

Sky loved her egg.
It made her feel warm and protected.

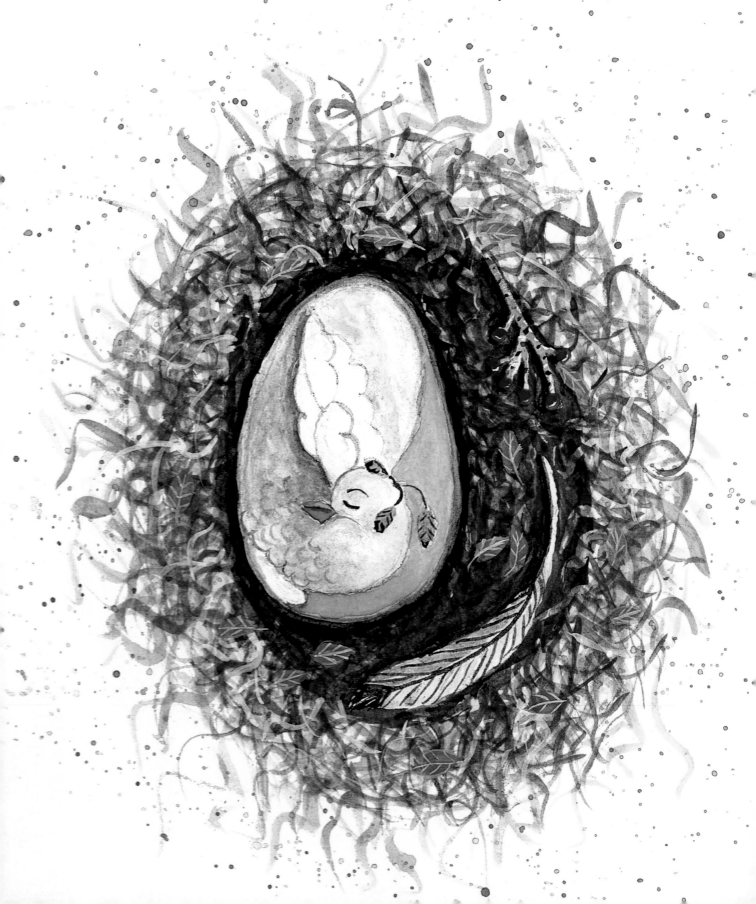

Sky thought her egg was the whole
entire world . . . until one day, she pecked her
way out of it.

She crawled out into her nest for the very first time. Things were much different outside her egg. The air was cooler, the light was brighter, and everything seemed to be made of twigs.

She saw two birds smiling down on her. They looked an awful lot like her, only much, much bigger.

"Who are you?" Sky cheeped.

"Why, we're your parents," replied her mother. **"And you're a bird, just like us."**

Sky loved sharing her nest with her parents. They made her feel safe and loved.

Sky thought her nest was the whole entire world . . .

until one day she fell out of it!

From the ground, Sky's nest seemed a million
miles away. She tried flapping her wings,
but she didn't know how to fly yet.

Sky needed help.

Her parents were out hunting worms,
so she decided to go looking for them.

Along her journey, Sky ran into a furry little creature she'd never seen before.

"Hello," she said. "My name's Sky. **Are you a bird like me?**"

"Nope," the creature replied. "I'm a squirrel. My friends call me Nutso."

Nutso did a funny little dance and wagged his bushy tail, which Sky thought was *very* neat.

"Pleasure to meet you, Nutso," she said. "Is there any chance you could fly me back to my nest?"

"I can't fly," replied Nutso. "But I am a very, *very-very* good climber. . . all you have to do is hold my tail and I'll carry you back to your nest."

Sky looked down at her wings and sighed, "I'm not very good at holding on to things."

"That's okay!" exclaimed Nutso. "I happen to know an expert flyer."

And so Sky set off with her new friend to find this expert flyer. Along the way, they crossed a great big field with high-high grass that towered over them.

"We're headed to the river!" cried Nutso. "Have you been there before?"

"Never ever," said Sky. "Until today, I thought my nest was the whole entire world."

"Hah!" laughed Nutso. "The world is a very, *very-very* big place, but the more you see, the smaller it seems."

At the river, Nutso led Sky to a bright patch of flowers where they met the most beautiful creature Sky had ever seen.

"Wow!" Sky exclaimed. **"Are you a bird like me?"**

"No," the creature replied. "I'm a butterfly, but you can call me Mona."

Mona flapped her wings and fluttered about, which Sky thought was *very* impressive.

"You sure are an expert flyer," said Sky. "Any chance you could fly me back to my nest?"

"I can fly, yes." replied Mona. "But surely I'm not strong enough to carry you myself."

Sky bowed her head and sighed, "I'll never make it home."

Mona flew down and wrapped her wing around Sky. "There, there, little one. One step at a time. I have an exceptionally tall friend who might be able to help. Come along now."

And so Sky set off with her new friends to find this exceptionally tall creature. Along the way, they passed over a giant mountain that overlooked the entire countryside.

"Have you ever been up this high?" asked Mona.

"Never ever," said Sky. "Until today, I thought my nest was the whole entire world."

Mona smiled. "The world is as big as you make it . . . and the higher you fly, the more you can see."

"But I can't fly," said Sky.

"Someday you will, little one. Someday."

At the bottom of the mountain, Mona led them to a watering hole where they met the tallest creature Sky had ever laid eyes on.

"Whoa!" Sky exclaimed. **"Are you a bird like me?"**

"No," the creature replied. "I'm a giraffe, but everyone calls me Stretch."

Stretch stretched his long-long neck and bit a leaf from the highest branch of a tall tree, which Sky thought was *very* nifty.

"You sure are exceptionally tall!" said Sky. "Do you think you're tall enough to lift me into my nest?"

"I don't see why not," replied Stretch. "I can reach just about anything."

"Hooray!" the animals cheered.

And so their journey began, back over the mountain, across the river, through the great big field, and finally to the tall-tall tree where it all began.

The four of them looked up at the tree in amazement. The nest was higher than they ever imagined.

"I'm not sure I can reach *that* high!" Stretch gulped.

"We just have to work together," said Mona.

"And remember to stay very, *very-very* calm!" added Nutso.

With Sky on his nose, Stretch stretched his

long

long

neck

up the

tall

tall

tree

as high as he could reach.

But the nest was still too high . . .

"I can't reach!" cried Stretch.

"I have an idea!" exclaimed Nutso.

In a flash, Nutso climbed Stretch's entire body and boosted Sky closer to the nest. He truly was a very, *very-very* good climber.

"Almost there!" cried Nutso.

But still, the nest was too high. . .

"It's too far!"
yelled Sky.
"I'll never make it!"

"Sure you will!"
Mona shouted.
"You'll have to fly the
rest of the way!"

Sky looked at Mona in disbelief.

"Fly?!"

she cried out.

"I'm not ready to fly! What if I fall again?"

"Nobody's sure when they're ready to fly," said Mona. "But if you let your fear stop you from trying, you'll end up on the ground instead of letting your wings take you far and high."

Sky was scared, but with the help of her new friends, she felt like she could do anything. And so, without further delay she yelled,

"Ready or not!"
and leapt into the air!

Sky flapped her wings
with all her might.

She flapped and flapped and
flapped some more, and just
when she thought she
couldn't flap any further,
she kept on flapping.

The nest was so close Sky could almost touch it!
But no matter how hard she tried, she couldn't
seem to reach it.

Until suddenly, she felt something lifting her
from below . . .

It was Mona!

She flew right underneath Sky
and gave her the final push she needed.

"We did it!"

the animals cheered as Sky
landed safely in her nest.

Just then, Sky's parents returned home. They both seemed very concerned.

"Sky!" cried Mother Bird. "Where have you been? We've been looking all over for you!"

"I fell out of the nest Mommy!" said Sky. "But my new friends helped me find my way home."

Sky's parents looked confused.

"Your new . . . *friends?*" asked Father Bird.

"Why yes!" Nutso smiled.

"Very, very-very good friends,
in fact."

"But Sky," said Father Bird.

"These animals . . . they're not birds like us."

"I know they're not birds like us,"
Sky told him.

"And they're
just the way
I like them!"

~~The End~~

Sky's the limit!

Noel Foy

Award-winning author of ABC Worry Free, Noel is a neuroeducator specializing in workshops and one-on-one coaching for kids and adults on anxiety, executive function and growth mindset. Noel's mission is to empower families and professionals with practical problem solving tools and playful stories that help manage stress, promote healthy change and maximize their unique potential. When Noel isn't writing, reading or working with clients, you will find her paddle boarding, kayaking or biking. She likes corny jokes and enjoys baking and cooking for family and friends.

Nicholas Roberto

A first time published author, Nicholas began writing children's books shortly after the birth of his daughter. His stories allow young readers to explore important, complex and challenging topics in a fun, kid-friendly way. He also enjoys writing music, eating ice cream, and coming home to his family after a long day of fly fishing.

Colleen Sgroi

Colleen dreamed of being an artist since she was a young girl. Her work is available world-wide on puzzles, calendars, prints and greeting cards, and her art has been included in films by major motion picture companies. Her illustrations in children's books have earned her a Moonbeam Best Illustrator Award and delight children everywhere. She teaches watercolor classes, inspiring others to find their own creativity. She loves to read, paint, walk in nature, and enjoys time with family and friends.

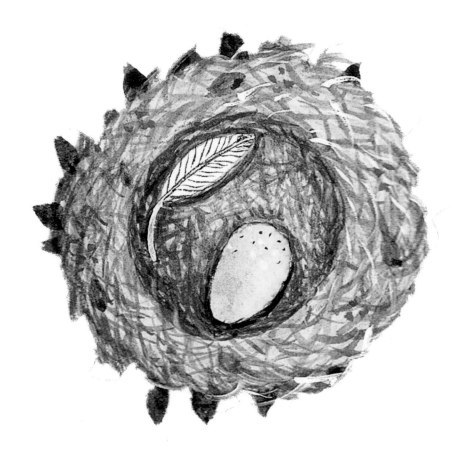

"Sometimes we need others to take us under their wings so we can spread our own." - Noel Foy

Made in United States
North Haven, CT
03 August 2022

22256396R00031